No Time for Hallie

ASPCA kids

PET RESCUE CLUB

No Time for Hallie

by Catherine Hapka
illustrated by Dana Regan

studio fun BOOKS

White Plains, New York • Montréal, Québec • Bath, United Kingdom

cover illustration by Steve James

Published by Studio Fun International, Inc.
44 South Broadway, White Plains, NY 10601 U.S.A. and
Studio Fun International Limited,
The Ice House, 124-126 Walcot Street, Bath UK BA1 5BG
Illustration 2015 Studio Fun International, Inc.
Text © 2015 ASPCA®
Studio Fun Books is a trademark of Studio Fun International, Inc.,
a subsidiary of The Reader's Digest Association, Inc.
Printed in China.
10 9 8 7 6 5 4 3 2 1
SL1/09/14

**The American Society for the Prevention of Cruelty to Animals (ASPCA®)
will receive a minimum guarantee from Studio Fun International, Inc. of $25,000
for the sale of ASPCA® products through December 2017.**

Comments? Questions? Call us at: 1-888-217-3346

Library of Congress Cataloging-in-Publication Data

Hapka, Catherine.
No time for Hallie / by Catherine Hapka ; illustrated by Dana Regan.
pages cm. -- (Pet Rescue Club;2)
Based on a real-life cat named Hallie.
Summary: "Zach's neighbors just had a new baby--and now they're threatening to
take their cat, Hallie, to the animal shelter. The kids have been volunteering there since
starting the Pet Rescue Club, and they know an older cat might have trouble getting
adopted. Can they convince the family to give their kitty another chance--or maybe find
someone who truly appreciates all that an older kitty has to offer?"
-- Provided by publisher.
ISBN 978-0-7944-3313-0 (paperback)
[1. Cats--Fiction. 2. Pets--Fiction. 3. Pet adoption--Fiction. 4. Animal shelters--Fiction.
5. Clubs--Fiction.] I. Title.
PZ7.H1996No 2015
[Fic]--dc23
2014028930

For Queen Rags and Buddy, who let me
stray onto their property.

C.H.

1
Bird Alert

"Good kitty, Mulberry." Janey Whitfield patted the fat orange tabby cat that had just jumped onto the sofa beside her. She giggled as he rubbed his face on her arm. "Your whiskers tickle! Aw, but that's okay— you love me, don't you?"

"He's just hoping you'll give him more food," Zach Goldman said with a laugh.

Mulberry was Zach's family's cat. Janey was at Zach's house, along with their friends Lolli Simpson and Adam Santos. Today was the first official meeting of the Pet Rescue Club—the group the four of them had decided to form after helping to rescue a neglected dog.

The meeting had started half an hour earlier. Zach's dad had brought out some snacks, and the four kids were supposed to be discussing how to organize their new group. But, they'd been too busy eating and playing with Mulberry to do much discussing so far.

Lolli selected a piece of cheese off the tray on the coffee table. "Did you add the stuff about the Pet Rescue Club to the blog?" she asked Janey.

"Yes." Janey pushed Mulberry away gently. Then she picked up her tablet computer and showed Lolli the screen.

Janey's blog had started as a way for kids around their town to share photos of their pets. Janey loved animals, but she couldn't have a pet of her own because her father was severely allergic to anything with fur or feathers. She'd thought that seeing pictures of lots of cute pets would be the next best thing to having her own.

Now the blog had another purpose, too. The Pet Rescue Club was going to use it to find animals that needed their help. So far Janey had written an update on the rescued dog and added a paragraph telling people to send in information on any animal that might need their help.

"Okay," Adam said. "So we put something on the blog. Now what?"

Adam was a very practical person. He was so responsible that he already had a successful pet-sitting business, even though he was only nine. People all over town paid him to come to their houses to feed and walk their dogs while they were at work or on vacation.

Janey didn't answer Adam right away. Mulberry was kneading his front paws on her leg and purring. Janey rubbed the cat's head and smiled.

"I wish I could have a cat like Mulberry," she said.

"Yeah, Mulberry is great!" Lolli leaned over to pet the cat. Mulberry turned around and butted his head against her arm.

Janey giggled. "And he's so cute! Here, Mulberry—want a cracker?"

"Don't give him that," Zach said quickly. "It's onion flavored and cats shouldn't eat onion—it's bad for them."

"Really?" Janey wasn't sure whether to believe him. Zach was always joking around and playing pranks on people. Still, she didn't want to hurt Mulberry if Zach was being serious for once. She pulled the cracker away and glanced at Adam. "Is that true? Are onions bad for cats?"

Adam shrugged. "Probably. I know dogs aren't supposed to eat onions."

"Why are you asking him? Don't you believe me?" Zach asked Janey. "My mom's a vet, you know. She's taught me lots of stuff like that."

Before Janey could answer, a pair of twelve-year-old boys raced into the room.

They were identical twins. Both of them were tall and skinny with wavy dark hair and the same brown eyes as Zach. It was raining outside, and the boys' sneakers left wet tracks on the floor.

Janey knew the twins were two of Zach's three older brothers. She couldn't imagine living with that many boys!

"Check it out," one of the twins said, pointing at Janey. "Little Zachie has a girl-friend!"

"No way—he has two girlfriends! Way to go, little bro!" the other boy exclaimed with a grin.

"Shut up!" Zach scowled at them. "And go away. We're trying to have a meeting here."

One of the twins stepped over and grabbed Mulberry off the sofa. "Yo, Mulberry," he said, cuddling the cat. "Are these girls bothering you?"

"Mulberry likes us," Lolli said with a

smile. "He's like the mascot of the Pet Rescue Club."

"Okay." The twin dropped Mulberry on the sofa again. The cat sat down and started washing his paw.

"Grab the umbrella and let's go," the other twin said. "The guys are waiting for us outside."

One of the twins grabbed an umbrella off a hook by the back door. Then they raced back out of the room.

"Sorry about that," Zach muttered. "They are so annoying."

"They're not so bad." Lolli smiled. She got along with everybody—even obnoxious boys. "Anyway, what were we talking about?"

"About how cats can't eat onion," Zach

said. "They shouldn't have chocolate, either. Did you know that?" He stared at Janey.

She shrugged. "No. That's interesting."

"Yeah," Lolli agreed. "There's lots to know about having a pet! When we first got Roscoe, I thought all he needed was a bowl of water and some dog food. But there's a lot more to it than that!"

Roscoe was the Simpsons' big, lovable dog. Lolli and her parents had found him at the Third Street Shelter a few years earlier. He was a mix of Labrador retriever, rottweiler, and who knew what else.

"I have an idea," Janey said. "You already said Mulberry was our club mascot. We should make Roscoe a mascot, too. We can post their pictures on the blog to make it official."

"Good idea," Lolli said. "I have a cute picture of Roscoe we can use."

"We should take a picture of Mulberry riding on my skateboard," Zach said. "That would be cool!"

"Veto," Janey replied.

Zach frowned at her. "Can't you just say no like a normal person?" he said. "Oh, wait, I forgot—you're not normal."

Janey ignored him. "Veto" was her new favorite word. Janey liked finding interesting words and using them. Saying veto was her new way of saying no.

"Hey Janey," Adam spoke up. "I think I heard your tablet ping."

"Really?" Janey had dropped her tablet

on the sofa. Now Mulberry was sitting on it. She pulled the tablet out from under the cat. "Sorry, Mulberry. That might be an animal who needs our help!"

Lolli leaned over her shoulder. "What does it say?"

"It's not a posting on the blog," Janey said. "It's alerting me to a new e-mail."

She clicked into her e-mail account. The message was from a classmate named Leah. Janey read it quickly.

Hi Janey,

I heard you're helping animals now. I need help! I just got home from my soccer practice and found out my pet canary is missing!

2
Runaway Cat?

"Oh, no!" Janey exclaimed, reading the e-mail again.

"What's wrong?" Adam asked.

"The e-mail is from Leah," Janey said. "She says her canary is missing!"

"Leah has a canary?" Lolli said. "I didn't know that."

"I didn't either. But if it's missing, we should try to help her find it," Janey said. "Zach, can I use the phone?"

"Sure, that'll be five dollars, please," Zach said.

Janey ignored the joke. She rushed into

the kitchen and grabbed the phone. Leah had put her number at the end of the e-mail.

"Janey?" Leah said from the other end of the line. "I was hoping you'd call. I'm so worried about Sunny!"

"What happened?" Janey asked.

"I must have forgotten to latch his cage after I fed him this morning before school." Leah sounded upset. "When I got home, the cage door was open and Sunny was nowhere in sight!"

"Oh, no," Janey exclaimed.

"That's not even the worst part," Leah went on. "My bedroom window was open! What if he flew outside? I might never find him!"

Janey glanced at Lolli, Adam, and Zach. They had followed her into the kitchen and were all listening to her half of the conversation.

"Don't worry, Leah," Janey said. "The Pet Rescue Club is on it! We'll be right over."

She hung up and told the others what Leah had said. "I don't like the idea of keeping birds cooped up in cages," Lolli said uncertainly. "Shouldn't they be free to fly around?"

"I don't know," Janey said. "But Leah sounded really worried."

"Then we should help her," Lolli said.

"Definitely," Zach agreed, and Adam nodded.

Mulberry had followed Janey into the kitchen, too. He rubbed against her legs. Then, suddenly, he meowed and rushed over to the screen door leading outside.

"Mulberry, what are you doing?" Lolli asked.

"Look!" Adam pointed. "There's another cat out there!"

Janey saw it, too. A cute black cat with big green eyes was looking in at them from outside!

"Where did that cat come from?" Lolli wondered.

"I don't know." Janey stepped closer and peered at the cat. "It's not wearing a collar or tags. But it looks healthy—just wet from the rain."

"I think I know where that cat lives," Zach said. "I've seen her in the window of a house across the street."

Lolli looked concerned. "Uh oh. What if she slipped out when her owners weren't looking? They'll be worried sick."

Adam nodded. "We should take her home."

"Yeah." Zach grinned. "This is the perfect chance for the Pet Rescue Club to rescue another pet!"

Janey felt impatient. "Okay, but hurry," she said. "Leah is waiting, remember?"

Zach ran to tell his father where they were going. Then the kids all went outside. Zach had to nudge Mulberry away from the door to stop him from following them.

The black cat was just as friendly as Mulberry. She rubbed against Lolli's legs and purred.

"Good kitty," Lolli said. "Can I pick you up?"

The cat purred louder. "I think she's saying yes," Janey said with a smile.

Lolli picked up the cat. "Which house is it?" she asked, squinting in the light rain.

"That one." Zach pointed to a white house with black shutters. "My parents have met the people who live here, but I don't know them at all. They only moved in last summer."

All four kids checked for traffic and then crossed the street. The cat stayed snuggled in Lolli's arms.

Janey led the way up the steps onto the front porch of the white house. There was no doorbell, but there was a brass knocker shaped like a seashell. Janey reached up and rapped the knocker two or three times.

They waited but there was no response. "Maybe they're not home," Adam said.

"Try knocking one more time," Lolli suggested.

"Here, let me do it. Janey knocks like

a girl." Zach pushed past the others and knocked harder. "There. If they're home, they should hear that."

Janey rolled her eyes at Lolli. Lolli just smiled.

Finally, there was the sound of footsteps from inside. Then the door swung open. A young woman was standing there. She was wearing sweatpants, and her hair was in a messy ponytail. A chubby baby with rosy cheeks was balanced on one hip.

"Oh, hello, kids," the woman said. "What are you doing with Hall Cat?"

"Hall Cat?" Lolli giggled. "Is that really her name?"

The young woman smiled back, though

she didn't look that happy. "Yes, that's her," she said. "Was she bothering you? Sometimes she's too friendly for her own good."

"No, she wasn't bothering us," Janey said. "We thought you might be looking for her, though. We found her outside." She smiled at the baby. He was staring at her with big, blue eyes.

"Yes, my husband let her out a little while ago." The young woman shifted the baby to her other hip. "Hall Cat is sweet, but ever since the baby came, she always seems to be underfoot." She wiped a spot of drool off the baby's chin. "I'm afraid I might trip over her and drop him."

"Oh." Janey looked at Hall Cat. The cat was still purring away in Lolli's arms, looking content and calm. "Um, maybe you didn't know, but being outside can be dangerous for a house cat. She could get hit by a car, or—"

"This is a quiet neighborhood," the young mother broke in. "Anyway, we had

to do something. What if she scratched the
baby while she was trying to play with him?
I can't take that chance."

She sounded so worried that Janey
couldn't help feeling sorry for her. But Janey

was worried about Hall Cat, too.

"Maybe you could keep the baby's door shut," she said. "Or—"

Just then the baby let out a loud gurgle. The young woman glanced at him.

"Thanks for being so concerned about Hall Cat, kids," she said. "But trust me, being outside is the best option we have right now. My husband and I don't want to take her to the shelter, so she'll just have to adjust."

"The shelter?" Zach sounded alarmed.

"But—" Janey began.

Suddenly the baby opened his mouth and started to wail. His mother winced, then hugged him to her, rocking him back and forth.

"Sorry, I really have to go," she said. "You can leave Hall Cat on the porch if you want—she seems to like it there. Bye now!"

Before Janey could come up with another way to change the woman's mind, the door swung shut.

3
Search and Rescue

"I still don't think we should have left Hall Cat outside," Zach said. It was a few minutes later, and the Pet Rescue Club was halfway to Leah's house. She only lived a few blocks away in the same neighborhood.

"I know." Janey shrugged. "But what else could we do? Break into her owners' house and sneak her back in?"

"We're supposed to be the Pet Rescue Club." Lolli kicked at a stone on the sidewalk. "We should try to figure out how to help Hall Cat."

"We will," Janey said. "Right after we help Leah find her bird."

She felt sorry for Hall Cat, too. But she was even more worried about Leah's canary.

Soon the Pet Rescue Club was ringing Leah's doorbell. Leah answered right away. She was a tall, skinny girl with freckles and glasses. Normally she was always smiling or laughing, but today she looked anxious and sad.

"Thanks for coming," she said. "Come in and I'll show you Sunny's cage."

Janey and the others went inside. Leah's four-year-old brother was sitting on the living room floor playing with a toy car. Two cats were watching him. One was a gray tabby, and the other was mostly white with brown and orange patches.

"Cute kitties," Lolli told Leah.

"Thanks." Leah barely glanced at the cats as she headed for the stairs. Janey guessed that she was too worried about Sunny to think about anything else.

The Pet Rescue Club followed Leah to her bedroom upstairs. The room was painted pale yellow with white trim. Along one wall was a bird cage. It was very tall, with several perches, a mirror, and colorful hanging toys.

"Wow." Lolli sounded impressed as she stepped closer for a better look. "This is a really nice cage!"

"Thanks," Leah said with a sad sigh. "Sunny loves it—at least I thought he did."

"It's so big," Zach commented. "Is it really all for one little bird?"

"Yes." Leah touched the cage. "Canaries need lots of room to fly. That's why Sunny's cage is so big."

"Really? That's interesting." Janey read everything she could about animals. But she didn't know that much about pet birds. "So you don't have any other canaries to keep Sunny company? Do you think that's why he flew away?"

Lolli nodded. "That makes sense. Maybe he was looking for a friend."

"Dogs like having other dogs around," Adam agreed.

"Actually, male canaries do better living alone," Leah said. "And like I said, Sunny seemed really happy. I don't know why he'd try to escape!"

"We should try to find him." Adam walked over to the window and looked out. "Maybe he's still in your backyard."

All five of them hurried downstairs and out the back door. For the next half hour, they searched Leah's backyard. The yard was pretty big, and had lots of shrubs and flowers. Janey didn't like getting her hands dirty, but she was willing to do it to help an animal. She pulled back the branches of a prickly rose bush, looking for a flash of yellow. But there was no sign of Sunny.

"Here, birdie, birdie!" Zach called. He whistled loudly.

"Not like that," Leah corrected. "He likes it when I whistle to him like this."

She let out a soft, musical whistle. Janey tried to imitate it, and couldn't do it. But Adam imitated the whistle perfectly!

"Dude!" Zach said with a laugh. "You sound like a canary! I always knew you were a birdbrain!"

"Quit joking around," Janey told him. "We need to find Sunny before it gets dark."

"I know." Zach shot a look at Leah. "Sorry. I'll look over there behind the shed."

Another twenty minutes passed with no sign of Sunny. Finally, the back door opened and Leah's mom looked out.

"Leah, are you out there?" she called.

"Sorry, but it's time for your friends to go home now. You need to set the table for dinner."

"But we haven't found Sunny yet!" Leah sounded frantic.

"I'm sorry, honey." Her mother did sound sorry, but she also sounded firm. "Maybe Sunny will find his way home on his own. There's nothing else you can do right now."

Leah sighed as her mother disappeared. "I'm so worried," she told Janey and the others, her voice quavering. "Poor little Sunny! He's not used to being out on his own."

"I know." Janey put an arm around her shoulders. "Try not to worry. The Pet Rescue Club will figure something out. I promise."

Zach hated waking up early. He always felt sleepy until almost lunchtime.

But the next morning when he looked out his bedroom window, he felt wide-awake right away. A small black shape was sitting on the sidewalk in front of his house.

"Hall Cat," Zach murmured. He tapped on the glass, but Hall Cat didn't hear him. She was watching a bird pecking at the grass nearby.

Moments later, Zach was dressed and heading for the door. He almost tripped over Mulberry, who was sleeping on the kitchen floor.

"Where are you going, dork?" his oldest brother, Josh, called out.

"Back in a sec," Zach said without slowing down.

Hall Cat came running when she saw Zach. She purred as he picked her up. Her fur felt soft and warm.

"Good girl," Zach whispered, tickling her chin. "I'm going to take you home, okay?"

Hall Cat kept purring. Zach carried her across the street. Even before he knocked on the door, he could hear the baby crying inside. A young man with a goatee answered Zach's knock.

"Hi," Zach said. "I found your cat outside."

The man peered at him. "You're one of the boys from across the street, right?" he said. "Hi there. Oh, and don't worry about Hall Cat. She likes it outside."

"Maybe," Zach said. "But it's dangerous out there. Um, you know, cars and stuff." He tried to remember what else he'd heard Janey and the others say.

"No, it's cool, seriously." The man said smiling, but he looked distracted. "We've been putting her out whenever the baby's awake, and she's been fine."

Zach squeezed Hall Cat a little tighter, making her wiggle. He didn't want the man to close the door and leave Hall Cat outside. But Zach wasn't sure what to say to stop him. He wished Janey was there—she always had lots of things to say. Or Adam, who knew so much about taking care of animals. Or Lolli—people seemed to like talking to her, even grownups.

"Um, how long have you had Hall Cat?" Zach blurted out.

The man glanced over his shoulder as another loud wail came from somewhere inside. "Quite a while," he said. He chuckled. "Longer than I've had my wife, actually."

"Really?" Zach said.

The man reached out to scratch Hall Cat under the chin, which made her purr even louder. "I got her in college actually," he said.

"I was living in a fraternity house and found her huddled under the front porch. She was super friendly, but none of our neighbors knew where she came from. So we kept her." He smiled. "She sort of became our fraternity mascot and visited everyone who lived on my hall. That's why we called her Hall Cat. After I graduated she stayed with me and the name had stuck."

"That's pretty funny," Zach said with a grin.

The man grinned back. "Anyway, when I got married a few years later, Hall Cat came to live with us. My wife had never had a pet before, but she's always liked Hall Cat." He sighed and glanced over his shoulder again as the baby let out a loud squawk somewhere inside. "But now, with the new baby, she's just a little overwhelmed and worried about what might happen, you know?"

Zach didn't really know what the man meant by that. Before he could ask, he heard a loud wheezing and clanking sound from the far end of the block.

"Oops," he said. "That's the school bus. Gotta go!"

He leaned to one side, tossing Hall Cat

gently past the man into the house. "Hey!" the man exclaimed, sounding surprised.

But Zach didn't stick around to find out whether the man threw Hall Cat back out or let her stay in. His backpack was still at home, and he'd have to run if he wanted to grab it before the bus got there.

4

Questions and Answers

When Janey got to school, she headed to Leah's cubby before even visiting her own. Leah was there putting her books away.

"Did you find him?" Janey asked.

As soon as Leah turned around, Janey could guess the answer. Leah still looked sad and worried.

"No," Leah said with a loud sigh. "I got up early this morning to search in the yard some more, but all I saw out there were wild birds and a few squirrels."

"Oh." Janey chewed her lower lip. "Okay, try not to worry. I'll figure something out, I promise."

She found Lolli at her cubby, which was right next to Janey's. Janey told her friend what she'd just found out from Leah.

"That's too bad," Lolli said. "Leah must be so worried."

"She is. And so am I." Janey noticed that Lolli didn't seem to be listening very carefully. She was looking at something over Janey's shoulder. When Janey looked that way, all she saw was one of their classmates, a girl named Brooke.

"Have you noticed that Brooke doesn't seem like her normal self?" Lolli whispered.

"Not really," Janey said. "What do you mean?"

"She's usually so happy and outgoing. But lately she's been a lot quieter. Today it even looks like she's been crying!" Lolli took a step toward Brooke. "I think I'll go ask her if anything's wrong."

"Wait!" Janey said. "We need to figure out what to do about Sunny."

It was too late. Lolli didn't hear her, because she was already hurrying toward Brooke. Letting out a sigh, Janey followed.

"Hi, Brooke," Lolli said when she reached the other girl. "Are you okay?"

Brooke was short with long, black hair. Right now her hair was hanging over her face, hiding one of her brown eyes. But the eye Janey could see looked sad.

"I'm fine," Brooke said.

"Are you sure?" Lolli put a hand on Brooke's arm. "You seem kind of upset or something. If you need someone to talk to…"

"No, really, I'm fine." Brooke said again. "I have to go."

Grabbing one more book out of her cubby, she rushed off. Lolli and Janey stared after her.

"She's definitely not fine," Lolli said. "Should we follow her and try to talk to her again?"

"Veto," Janey said. "We're supposed to be helping pets, not people, remember?"

Just then Zach zoomed up to the girls on his skateboard. "Hi," he greeted them breathlessly.

"You're not supposed to ride your skate-board in the halls," Janey reminded him. "Don't let the teachers see you, or you'll have to stay after school. And we'll probably need everyone in the Pet Rescue Club to help search for Leah's canary again today."

"Never mind that bird," Zach said. "We need to help Hall Cat. I found her outside again this morning."

He told Janey and Lolli what the neighbor had said. Lolli shook her head.

"I was hoping they'd let her come back inside after we talked to the baby's mom yesterday," she said. "I guess not."

"We need to convince them to take better care of Hall Cat," Zach said. "Or else she might get hit by a car or something!"

"I'm sure her owners don't want that,"

Lolli said. "They seem nice. Just kind of busy with the new baby."

Janey nodded. "Okay, we should definitely figure out a way to help Hall Cat," she said. "But what about Sunny? If a cat is in danger outside, what about a tiny little bird? I think we need to find him first, then come up with a plan for Hall Cat."

"No way," Zach said. "Hall Cat needs us right now!"

"Wow," Lolli said. "Now that we started the Pet Rescue Club, there are even more pets to help than I expected! I guess we need to figure out how to help two pets at once."

"Hall Cat will be fine for a few days," Janey argued. "There really isn't much traffic in our neighborhood."

"What if she wanders off and gets lost, though?" Zach argued back. "Or gets attacked by a mean dog, or eats something she shouldn't? There are some plants and stuff that are poisonous to cats—not just onions, either."

Before Janey could respond, she saw Adam walking toward them with Ms. Tanaka, their homeroom teacher. Ms. Tanaka was young and friendly and smiled a lot, which made her almost everyone's favorite teacher.

"Hi!" Janey called. "How's Truman?"

Truman was the dog that had inspired Janey and the others to start the Pet Rescue Club. With the help of the local animal shelter, the kids had worked together to save him from a neglectful home and help him find a new home with Ms. Tanaka.

"Truman is great!" Ms. Tanaka said with a smile. "I took him for a nice, long walk after school yesterday."

"That's awesome," Janey said. Hearing how well Truman was doing made her more determined than ever to help more animals —starting with Sunny.

Ms. Tanaka waved and headed into her classroom. After she was gone, Janey and the others told Adam what they'd been talking about.

"Okay, it sounds like we have two pets who need our help right away," Adam said. "Maybe we should divide and conquer."

"What do you mean?" Janey asked.

Adam shrugged. "There are four of us," he pointed out. "Maybe Zach should talk to Hall Cat's owners after school, and Janey and Lolli can go look for the lost bird."

"What about you?" Lolli asked.

"I'll come help whoever needs me after I take care of my clients," Adam said.

Janey thought about Adam's idea. It made sense. Zach was too hyper to be much help searching for Sunny, anyway.

"Wait, so I have to go talk to Hall Cat's owners all by myself?" Zach asked. "I was hoping you guys could help me convince them."

"Adam can come help you later," Janey said. "I think his plan could work. Let's do it!"

5

Kitty and Cats

Lolli usually liked school. But that day, she was happy when the final bell rang. She was worried about both of the pets that the Pet Rescue Club was trying to help. Besides, she'd had an idea she wanted to tell Janey and Leah about.

She walked out of the classroom with the two of them. "Ready to go to Leah's house and look for Sunny?" Janey asked her. "I already called my mom to come and drive us there so we don't have to wait for the bus."

"Actually, I was thinking about something," Lolli said. She turned to Leah. "Did you check with the Third Street Shelter after Sunny went missing? Maybe someone found him and took him there."

"I called them yesterday," Leah said. "Nobody had brought him in yet." She bit her lower lip. "Anyway, I doubt anyone except me could catch Sunny."

Janey nodded. "It's okay. He's probably still in your yard. We'll find him."

Janey sounded very certain. Lolli had heard her friend sound that way a lot. Sometimes it meant that Janey was so busy thinking about her own plans that she wasn't paying enough attention to what other people were saying. So Lolli cleared her throat and talked a little louder.

"Even if nobody could catch him, some-body might call the shelter to report seeing him," she said. "If you want, I'll call home and ask if it's okay for me to walk over there and check."

The animal shelter was only a few blocks from school. Lolli's parents had let her walk there before, so she guessed they would say yes today, too.

"That's a good idea," Leah said. "If some-one reported seeing Sunny, it will help us figure out if he's still in my backyard or if he flew somewhere else."

Janey blinked at Lolli. "Oh. Yeah, I guess that's true. Are you sure you don't mind going to the shelter by yourself?"

"It will be fine," Lolli said. "One of my parents can probably pick me up there and drive me over to meet you guys at Leah's house."

She said good-bye to Janey and Leah, then headed for the school office to call home. As she'd guessed, her father said it was okay to walk to the shelter. He promised to meet her there in a few minutes to pick her up.

As she walked down the sidewalk, Lolli spotted Brooke walking just ahead of her. Brooke's head was down, and her steps were slow.

"Hey, Brooke!" Lolli broke into a jog to catch up. "Wait up. Are you walking toward town, too?"

Brooke stopped and waited. "Uh huh. I'm supposed to meet my dad at his office," she said. "Why are you walking this way? I thought you lived on a farm."

"I do." Lolli and the other girl both started walking again. "But today I'm going to the animal shelter." She told Brooke about the Pet Rescue Club and their search for Sunny.

"Wow," Brooke said. "That's cool that you guys are trying to help animals."

"Thanks." Lolli smiled at her. "Do you walk to your dad's office every day after school?"

"No, I usually take the bus." Brooke sighed. "But everything is different lately."

Lolli leaned closer. "What do you mean? Does it have to do with why you look so sad?" She reached over and gave Brooke's arm a squeeze. "Sorry, my parents tell me I'm too nosy. I just want to help if I can."

Brooke sniffled. Then she took a deep breath.

"You're nice, Lolli," she said. "I guess I can tell you. My grandpa fell and hurt himself a few weeks ago."

Lolli gasped. "Oh, no! Is he okay?"

"Not really." Brooke shrugged. "I mean, his broken hip is getting better, but he still can't walk by himself or go up and down the stairs. So instead of letting him go home after he got out of the hospital, they sent him to another place."

"Another place?" Lolli wrinkled her nose. "What do you mean?"

"It's called an assisted care facility," Brooke said. "He has to live there while he does lots of physical therapy and stuff. Nobody is sure how long that will take."

"Wow." Lolli thought about her own grandfathers. Her dad's dad sold real estate, and her mom's dad was retired but still played golf or tennis almost every day. "No wonder you're upset."

"Not as upset as my grandma." Brooke kicked a stone on the sidewalk. "She's living in their house all by herself now. She says she's fine, but I can tell she's sad and lonely without Grandpa around."

"Oh, that's terrible." Lolli's eyes filled with tears at the thought of Brooke's grandma being so sad.

Brooke nodded. "That's why I'm going to my dad's office. I'm planning to spend lots of time with Grandma to help her feel less lonely. Dad is going to drive me over there today."

"That's nice. I bet she'll love seeing you," Lolli said. "Let me know if I can do anything to help, okay? I'm good at reading to people if she might like that, or I can bake her some cookies…"

Brooke looked thoughtful. "Grandma can read to herself just fine," she said. "But actually, maybe there is something you can do…"

"Kitty?" Lolli stuck her head into the cat room at the Third Street Shelter. "The guy at the front desk said you were in here."

Kitty look up and smiled, spitting out a strand of blond hair that was caught in her lip gloss. She was the Pet Rescue Club's favorite shelter worker.

"Hi, Lolli," Kitty said. "What brings you here today? I didn't see your name on the volunteer schedule." She winked. "Did you come to adopt another dog to keep Roscoe company?"

Lolli giggled. "I'd love to, but my parents would kill me." She stepped into the room to pet a cute tiger-striped cat that was wandering around while Kitty cleaned out her litter box. "Actually, I'm here on official Pet Rescue Club business."

She told Kitty about Sunny. By the time she was finished, Kitty was shaking her head.

"Sorry, no calls about a loose canary," she said. "I'll be sure to let you guys know right away if I hear anything, though."

"Thanks." Lolli leaned closer to the

cat, who had started purring as soon as Lolli started petting her. "Hey, I remember you from my first day volunteering here," Lolli cooed. "You're so cute! I can't believe nobody has adopted you yet."

Kitty nodded. "Yes, Tigs is adorable," she said. "But she's also ten years old, and unfortunately, most people don't want to take on a cat her age."

"Really?" Lolli couldn't help thinking about Hall Cat. Based on what her owner had told Zach, she was probably at least ten years old, too. "Why not?"

Kitty shrugged. "Older animals have a lot of love to give," she said. "But I guess it makes people sad to think they might not have an older pet for as long as a younger one. I don't know. But a cat of Tigs' age will be lucky if anyone even considers adopting her—no matter how cute and friendly she is."

Lolli nodded, feeling a flash of worry for Hall Cat. Her owners said they weren't planning to take her to the shelter. But what if they changed their minds?

They won't, she told herself firmly. I'm sure they'll decide to keep her—and keep her inside, too. After all, the Pet Rescue Club is on the case!

6
Different Strokes

"How many more clients do you have today?" Zach asked, feeling impatient. "I want to get to Hall Cat's house soon."

He'd decided to wait for Adam before starting his mission. Otherwise, he was afraid he wouldn't know what to say again. And that wouldn't help Hall Cat at all.

"Just one more," Adam said, pointing to a blue house up ahead. "It won't take long, since I just have to walk the dog and not feed it or anything."

"Really? Why, is the dog on a diet?" Zach grinned.

"Ha ha, very funny," Adam said. "It's because the owners just had twin babies."

"Twins?" Zach made a face. "I hope they're not anything like my obnoxious twin brothers."

Adam smiled. "Actually, these twins are pretty cute," he said. "But the mom has trouble walking the dog with both babies along, and the dad works all day in another town. So they hired me to walk the dog for them, at least until the twins are older."

"Oh." Zach thought about that. It reminded him of Hall Cat's owners, except they hadn't hired Adam to take care of their pet. They'd put her outside instead.

When Adam knocked on the door, a young woman with lots of dark curls and big brown eyes answered. Behind her, Zach could see a spacious living room. Two babies were playing with blocks on the rug. A large, fluffy collie was lying there watching them, but he jumped up and barked happily when he spotted Adam.

"Hi there, Brody." Adam rubbed the dog's ears as it rushed over to greet him. "Mrs. Cooper, this is my friend Zach Goldman. He's helping me today."

"Hi, Zach." Mrs. Cooper smiled as she handed Adam a leash. "Goldman—are you related to Brody's vet, Dr. Goldman?"

"Yeah, that's my mom," Zach said. He was used to having people ask about his mother. Almost all the pets in town went to her veterinary practice.

But he wasn't really thinking about his mom. He was still thinking about Hall Cat. He stared at Brody as Adam clipped the leash onto the dog's collar.

"Hey, Mrs. Cooper," Zach blurted out. "Did you think about making Brody live outside when you had your babies?"

Mrs. Cooper looked startled. Then she smiled and shook her head.

"No, not even for a second," she said, bending over to rub her dog's head. "Brody is part of the family. And in this family, that means living inside!"

"But isn't it a lot of work having a dog and twins?" Zach asked. "What if you trip over Brody or something?"

"I suppose it's a little extra work," Mrs. Cooper said, glancing over at the twins. "We had to make sure to introduce Brody to the babies slowly, and we always watch carefully when he's with them." She shrugged. "Any extra work is worth it, though."

"Come on, Zach," Adam said. "Brody is ready for his walk."

Zach kept thinking about what Mrs. Cooper had said as he wandered along after Adam and Brody. He was glad that Brody had such nice owners. But he was more worried than ever about Hall Cat. What could he and the rest of the Pet Rescue Club do to convince her owners to change their minds about keeping her outside?

⁓

"Do you think Sunny joined a flock of wild birds or something?" Janey asked, peering at a bird perched on a branch overhead.

She was in Leah's backyard. The two of them had been searching for Sunny all afternoon. First they'd looked in the back-yard. Then they'd checked the front yard, and then the empty lot across the street. Finally,

they'd returned to the backyard, since that was the closest to Leah's bedroom window.

"I doubt it," Leah said. "Male canaries are solitary. They like to have their own space."

"Really?" Janey pursed her lips. "Wait. Then why are you so sure he flew out the window?"

Leah shrugged. "I'm not sure. But I haven't heard him in the house since he disappeared. Or heard him singing, either."

"Okay," Janey said. "But if you were a tiny bird, and you were loose in a house with a couple of cats and a loud little kid, wouldn't you keep quiet?"

Leah's eyes widened. "You're right! I barely searched inside at all. I was so sure he flew out the window, I didn't even think about him being in the house."

Janey had been feeling discouraged. But now she was excited again. She might have just cracked the case of the missing canary!

"Come on, Leah." She headed for the back door. "Let's go search inside now!"

7

The Search is On

Soon Janey and Leah were searching inside Leah's house. Leah's little brother was taking a nap, and her mother was busy on the computer in the den, so the house was quiet. After a while, the gray tabby cat noticed what the two girls were doing and started following them.

"Scat, Buddy," Leah told the cat. "Trust me, Sunny doesn't want to see you right now."

The cat ignored her, rubbing against Janey's legs. Normally Janey loved cats just as much as she loved all animals. But right now seeing one of Leah's cats made her feel uneasy. Cats liked to hunt smaller animals— including birds. What if Leah's cats decided to hunt Sunny?

"We need to find Sunny fast," she said.

Leah glanced at the cat. "I know. But how? If he's scared and hiding, we might never find him!"

Janey thought for a second. "I've got it," she said. "You told us that Sunny likes it when you whistle to him, right?"

"Right," Leah replied. "It makes him happy, and he usually starts singing." She gasped. "Janey, you're a genius! Maybe if I whistle, Sunny will answer!"

"What are you waiting for?" Janey smiled. She liked being called a genius! "Start whistling!"

They walked around the house slowly, with Leah whistling a merry tune the whole way. Janey listened as hard as she could. Would Sunny answer?

"There!" she cried as they passed an open doorway leading into a bedroom. "I heard something—a whistle!"

"It's Sunny!" Leah exclaimed. She stepped into the room and whistled. Once again, there was a whistle in return!

Janey looked down at Buddy. The cat was still following the girls. He'd stopped and sat down in the bedroom doorway. But his ears were pricked toward the room, and his tail was twitching.

Leah stepped into the room and looked around. "I don't see him," she said. "He must be hiding."

There were lots of places to hide in the room. It seemed to be the place where Leah's family put everything that didn't have another place to go. There were a couple of bookshelves packed full of books and other stuff, a bed with tons of pillows, and lots of other odds and ends of furniture. Several cardboard boxes were stacked in one corner, and the half-open closet door barely contained all the clothes and other things inside. How were they ever going to find a tiny bird in there?

Once again, Janey started thinking hard. She looked around the room and spotted another door.

"Does that door open into your bedroom?" she asked Leah.

"Actually, it opens into the bathroom," Leah said. "I share it with this room—this is just a guest room, so the bathroom is mostly mine."

Janey nodded. Then she bent down and gently shoved Buddy into the hall. "Sorry, Buddy," she said as she shut the door in the cat's face. "But we don't need your help with this."

"What are you doing?" Leah asked. "Do you have an idea for how to get Sunny to come out? I'm still not sure he'll let me catch him, though." She looked worried. "He must be awfully scared if this is the first time he's sang in two days!"

"Don't worry, I have a plan." Janey hurried over and opened the door into the bathroom. She continued through the small room into Leah's bedroom. When she entered, Buddy was just strolling in from the hall. "Eh, eh, eh!" Janey scolded the cat gently. She scooped him up and deposited him back in the hallway. "Like I just told you, we don't need your help right now."

She closed the bedroom door, shutting the cat out. But she left the doors between the bathroom and the two bedrooms wide open.

"Okay," she said to Leah, who had followed her into her bedroom. "Now we need to put all of Sunny's favorite foods in his cage, and leave the door open. We'll sit very still, and you'll whistle to try to call him in."

Leah nodded. "I get it! We can lure him into his cage. It could work!"

They set Janey's plan into motion right away. Leah filled Sunny's food dishes with lots of tasty treats. Then she and Janey crouched down near the cage.

"Okay," Janey said. "Now, whistle!"

Leah took a deep breath and whistled her song. At first nothing happened. Janey started to feel worried. What if Sunny couldn't hear them from the other room?

She shifted her weight. Sitting still and being quiet weren't Janey's favorite things. But she knew that if she moved at the wrong time, she might scare Sunny. So she did her best to act like a statue.

"I don't know if this is going to work," Leah whispered. "I don't hear any—wait! There he is!"

Janey heard it, too. Sunny was singing again! And he sounded closer!

"Keep whistling," she whispered. "I think he's in the bathroom now!"

Leah nodded and whistled her song again. Sunny didn't answer this time. But a moment later Janey saw a flash of bright yellow zip in through the bathroom door. It was Sunny! The little canary flew over and perched on top of his cage.

Janey held her breath. Beside her, Leah stopped whistling. Janey could see that the other girl's fingers were crossed, and she guessed that they were both thinking the same thing. Would Sunny go back into his cage?

The next few minutes seemed to last about forty-two days, at least to Janey. But finally, Sunny hopped down onto the top of his cage door. He perched there for another few seconds, then flew right into the cage!

"Oh, Sunny!" Leah cried as she leaped up and snapped the door shut. "It's so good to have you home!"

The little bird pecked at his food. Then he let out a trill before going back to eating.

Janey grinned. "We did it!"

"You did it." Leah spun around and hugged her. "Thank you so much! I don't know what I would have done without you."

"It was nothing," Janey said modestly. "Just another successful case for the Pet Rescue Club."

8
Zach's Mission

"A toast to Janey!" Lolli cried, lifting her bottle of juice.

"And the Pet Rescue Club!" Adam added.

"And the Pet Rescue Club," Lolli agreed.

"Thanks, guys," Janey said with a smile. It was the next day at lunchtime. The four members of the Pet Rescue Club were sitting together in the school cafeteria. Actually, Janey, Lolli, and Adam had been sitting together since the beginning of the year. Zach had usually sat at a different table. Now he sat with them every day.

Usually there was no forgetting that, since he never stopped talking and joking around. But today he was being very quiet.

"What's wrong, Zach?" Janey asked, giving him a poke on the arm. "Aren't you excited that we helped another pet?"

Zach looked up. "Hip hip hooray," he said with a shrug. "I'm glad you found Leah's bird. But we haven't done anything to help Hall Cat yet."

Adam sipped his chocolate milk. "Yeah, it's too bad her owners weren't home yesterday when we went there."

"We'd better try again today," Zach said. "Let's meet up and go over there right after school."

"Veto," Janey said. "You guys can go

without me. I have to stay after school today for my flute lesson."

"Sorry, Zach, but I can't make it today, either," Lolli said. "I promised Brooke I'd bring Roscoe to visit her grandma."

"Oh, right," Janey said. Lolli had told the whole group about her talk with Brooke. When Lolli had offered to help, Brooke had explained that her grandmother was a lifelong animal lover. Since Lolli was a member of the Pet Rescue Club, Brooke had asked if she knew any animals who could visit the old lady to cheer her up. Lolli had immediately volunteered to bring her own dog, who was super friendly and loved going to new places.

Adam smiled. "The Pet Rescue Club is

already expanding," he said. "We started off as people helping animals. Now we're also animals helping people!"

Janey giggled. Adam didn't joke around nearly as much as Zach did, but the jokes he made were usually really funny.

"I guess that's true," Janey said. "After all, Roscoe is an honorary member, since he's one of our mascots. Maybe next time Mulberry can go for a visit!"

She glanced at Zach to see what he thought of that. But he didn't even seem to be listening.

He was looking at Adam. "I guess you can't come to Hall Cat's house right after school, either, right?" he said. "You probably have to take care of your clients."

"Right," Adam said. "I can come meet

you when I'm finished, though."

Lolli nodded. "I probably won't be at Brooke's grandma's house for that long," she said. "I'll come help with Hall Cat after I'm done, too."

"Me, three," Janey said. "I'll get my mom to drop me off there after my lesson."

"Okay." Zach looked a little happier. He reached for Janey's last carrot stick and popped it into his mouth. "You weren't going to eat that, were you?" he mumbled.

Zach stared out the living room window. He could see Hall Cat's house from there. He could also see Hall Cat. She was sleeping in her owners' driveway. Zach winced every time a car drove by, even though the cat wasn't that close to the road at the moment. But what if she decided to take a nap in the middle of the road next time?

Zach wondered how much longer it would be before his friends showed up. He'd lost his watch weeks ago, so he jumped up and hurried into the kitchen to check the clock on the microwave.

"No way!" he said out loud. He glanced at his oldest brother, who was fixing a sandwich. "Is that clock right?"

Josh glanced at him. "Why? Do you have an important business meeting?" Snorting with laughter, Josh picked up his sandwich and loped out of the kitchen.

Zach gritted his teeth. The clock had to be wrong! It was impossible that he'd only been home from school for half an hour. That meant his friends probably wouldn't be there for almost another hour!

He hurried back into the living room and looked outside. Hall Cat had woken up. She was sitting up and washing her paw.

"I can't wait any longer," Zach muttered. Yelling to his father that he was going out, he hurried across the street.

This time the baby's father opened the door again. His wife was sitting in a chair right behind him, trying to squeeze the baby's chubby foot into a tiny sock.

When the father saw Zach standing there holding Hall Cat, he sighed. "Hello again," he said. "Is Hall Cat getting into trouble?"

"Not yet," Zach said. "But she might if you keep putting her outside." He took a deep breath, trying to remember all the stuff Janey and the others had said, along with everything his mother had told him about outdoor cats when he'd tried to convince her that Mulberry wanted to go outside and chase mice. "She probably won't live as long being an outdoor cat. She could get hit by a car, or eat something poisonous, or get attacked by mean dogs or wild animals, or—"

"All right, all right," the father said. He sounded a little worried. "I know it's not ideal. But this is a safe neighborhood, and we're just trying to come up with a solution that works for everybody."

Zach took a step inside and set Hall Cat down on the floor. She wandered toward the baby and sniffed at his foot, which was dangling off the side of the chair.

"Careful, Hall Cat," the mother said. "Don't scare the baby." She glanced at her husband. "Put the cat back out, will you, honey?"

Zach didn't think the baby looked scared at all. He wondered if the woman had heard anything he'd just said. Zach's older brothers ignored him all the time, and Zach hated it. He was getting the same feeling now.

"Hall Cat's not scary, but I am!" he blurted out. Putting his thumbs in his ears, he waggled his fingers and made a funny face at the baby. "Ooga booga!"

He was only joking around, but the baby's face scrunched up. A second later he let out a loud wail.

"Oh, no!" the baby's mother exclaimed,

grabbing him and hugging him close. "It's okay, sweetie. Don't cry! Please, don't start crying again!"

"I'm sorry." Zach immediately felt guilty. "I was just kidding around. I didn't think that would actually scare him."

The father put a hand on his shoulder. "I know, kiddo. You couldn't know that the baby was up all night with an earache. We're all a little touchy right now, that's all."

"Sorry," Zach muttered again, feeling his face go red. "I guess I'll go."

The mother glanced up at him. "Yes, maybe you'd better," she said with a sigh. "Please take Hall Cat back outside on your way, all right?"

9
Roscoe Helps Out

Lolli was having a great time at Brooke's grandmother's house. Her father had met her in the car with Roscoe right after school. He'd dropped Lolli, Brooke, and Roscoe off at a tidy two-story house just a few blocks from Zach's place.

"Grandma's expecting us," Brooke had told Lolli as Mr. Simpson drove off. "She can't wait to meet Roscoe. She hasn't had a dog in a few years, but she loves them."

Brooke was right. Brooke's grandmother

had been thrilled to see them—especially Roscoe.

"Oh, aren't you a big lug of a fellow?" she'd cooed, walking out onto the front stoop to rub Roscoe all over. The dog had enjoyed every second of the attention, wiggling from head to foot with his tail wagging nonstop.

Finally the old woman had glanced up with a smile. She looked like an older version of Brooke, with friendly brown eyes behind wire-rimmed glasses.

"I'm sorry, where are my manners?" she'd exclaimed, ushering Lolli, Roscoe, and Brooke into her house. It was nice and cool inside, with lots of framed family photos decorating the walls and the scents of lavender and lemon in the air. "You must be Lolli. It's lovely to meet you. You can call me Grandma Madge if you like."

"Okay." Lolli smiled back, liking the woman already. "It's nice to meet you, too, Grandma Madge. This is Roscoe."

"Oh, I know." Grandma Madge rubbed the dog's ears. "Brookie told me all about both of you. Is it true you live on a farm?"

"Yes," Lolli said. "It's not a very big farm, but it's big enough for the three of us. My parents grow all kinds of organic vegetables, and sometimes they make cheese from our goats' and sheep's milk."

"Wonderful! Roscoe must love having a whole farm to patrol," Grandma Madge said.

Brooke flopped onto a comfortable-looking sofa. "Grandma loves big dogs," she told Lolli. "Isn't that right, Grandma?"

"Absolutely." Grandma Madge sat on a chair and patted her knees. Roscoe came over and laid his big, blocky head on the woman's lap. His tongue flopped out, and drool dribbled onto Grandma Madge's slacks.

"Oops," Lolli said. "Sorry about that. He drools when he's happy."

"Oh, don't be silly." The old woman

laughed. "What's a little drool among friends? Why, I once had a Saint Bernard who could sling drool farther than you could toss a ball…"

After that, she was off and running, telling the girls a whole series of stories about the dogs and cats she'd known throughout her long life. She'd always had at least one pet around for as long as she could remember.

"…and of course, Brookie remembers Muffin," she finished, glancing at her granddaughter.

Brooke nodded. "She was this awesome dog Grandma had when I was little," she told Brooke. "Muffin used to let me dress her up, even though she was even bigger than Roscoe."

Lolli laughed. "She sounds cool," she said. "What kind of dog was she?"

"Nobody was ever quite sure." Grandma Madge chuckled. "She was just this gorgeous big black and tan mixed breed who could shed enough fur in a week to make three new dogs. We used to take a survey at parties to see what mix of breeds people thought she might be. We got everything from Great Dane to German shepherd to giant schnauzer!"

"Whatever breeds she was, Muffin was the best," Brooke said.

"Yes, she was quite a dog," Grandma Madge agreed with a faraway look in her eyes. She fondled Roscoe's ears. "She passed on a few years ago now."

"Did you think about getting another

dog?" Lolli asked. "Or did you miss Muffin too much?"

"Oh, I missed her all right. And yes, I thought about getting another. But by then, I was feeling too old to handle another large dog."

"I tried to talk them into getting a smaller dog, like a beagle or something," Brooke put in. "Or maybe a cute little kitten from the shelter."

Grandma Madge nodded. "We did consider it, but my husband was starting to get unsteady on his feet around that time. It just didn't seem worth the risk of him tripping over a new pet." She sighed. "Plus, I'm not sure I have the energy anymore for a lively puppy or kitten."

"That's too bad," Lolli said. "I can't

imagine not having animals around." She thought about Leah's pet canary. "Did you think about getting a pet that doesn't run around the house?"

"You mean, like a bird or something?" Grandma Madge shrugged. "That just wouldn't be the same."

She looked sad for a moment. Then Roscoe reached up and slurped her face with his large tongue, knocking her glasses askew.

"Oh!" Lolli exclaimed as she reached for her dog. "Roscoe, no! Bad dog!"

But Grandma Madge was laughing as she took off her glasses and rubbed them on her shirt. "No, don't scold him," she told Lolli. "He's just doing what dogs do. And I love it!" She stuck her glasses back on and stroked Roscoe's head.

Lolli smiled, though she felt a little bit sad herself. Grandma Madge loved animals—that was obvious. It was too bad she'd been without a special pet of her own for so long.

But thinking about Leah's bird had reminded Lolli about the Pet Rescue Club. That made her remember that she'd promised to meet her friends to talk to Hall Cat's owners. She stood up.

"I'm sorry, I should probably go," she told Grandma Madge and Brooke. "But maybe Roscoe and I could stop by and visit again another time?"

"I'd love that." Grandma Madge hugged Roscoe. "Please, come by whenever you like." She winked. "You too, Lolli."

Soon Lolli was hurrying down the sidewalk. "I wonder if the others are already at Hall Cat's house," she said to Roscoe. "Should we go to Zach's house first to see if he's there, or..."

She let her voice trail off. Just ahead, Hall Cat's front door had just swung open. A second later, Zach stepped out, looking red-faced and upset as he clutched Hall Cat in his arms.

10
Lolli's Big Idea

"Zach!" Lolli rushed over as Zach stumbled toward the sidewalk, still holding Hall Cat. "What happened? Where are the others?"

"Not here yet," Zach said. Then he blinked. "Wait, yes they are."

Lolli looked around. Adam was hurrying down the sidewalk toward them. Janey was just climbing out of her mother's car at the curb.

"Sorry I'm late," Adam said breathlessly. He looked at Hall Cat. "Did you talk to her owners?"

"Sort of," Zach said.

Janey rushed up. "Hi, Roscoe," she greeted the dog as he jumped around happily. "What's going on, you guys? Oh! Hall Cat is still outside."

Zach nodded. "I tried talking to them," he said. "They didn't listen."

"Why didn't you wait for us?" Janey said. "Come on, let's go try again."

"I don't think that's a good idea." Zach stroked Hall Cat's back, making her purr. "They seem kind of, um, distracted right now."

Adam shook his head. "It seems like those people just don't have time for a pet," he said. "Cats are a little easier to take care of than dogs. But cats need attention, too!"

"I know, right?" Zach tickled Hall Cat under her chin. "Especially Hall Cat. She's so sweet! I wish I could take her home. I bet they would let me." He sighed. "Unfortunately, my parents definitely wouldn't let me."

Lolli stared at Hall Cat. Then she stared at her friends. She was starting to get an idea...

"I wish I could take Hall Cat home, too," Janey said. "But you know about my dad's allergies. Maybe you could take her, Adam?"

"Sorry, I can't," Adam said. "My family's landlord doesn't allow any pets. That's why I don't have a dog, remember?"

"Really?" Janey blinked at him. "Oh. I never knew that."

Zach rolled his eyes. "That's because you never stop talking long enough to listen to anybody else."

Janey looked wounded. "I do too!"

"Don't start arguing," Adam told them. "We're supposed to be figuring out a way to help Hall Cat, remember? Maybe Lolli could take her home. Her parents wouldn't even notice another animal on the farm, right?"

Zach brightened. "That's a great idea!"

"Lolli?" Janey poked Lolli on the shoulder. "Why aren't you saying anything?"

"I'm thinking," Lolli said. "I might have an idea for a way to help Hall Cat."

"Really?" Adam said. "You mean you thought of something to convince her people to keep her inside?"

Lolli shrugged. "No," she said. "But maybe that's not the point. Even if they kept her inside, they just don't seem that interested in her anymore."

"So you're going to ask your parents if you can keep her?" Zach asked.

"Me? No." Lolli smiled. "But I might know someone who would appreciate her a lot more than her owners do."

"Really? Who?" Janey asked.

Lolli pointed down the block. "Brooke's grandma," she said. "She loves animals, but she can't have a big dog or a hyper puppy or frisky kitten."

Zach glanced down at the cat purring in his arms. "Hall Cat isn't hyper."

"Right." Lolli smiled. "Come on, let's go ask her owners if they'd be willing to give her up to a good home."

When the baby's father answered the door, he looked annoyed at first. But when he heard the kids' question, he looked thoughtful.

"Do you really know someone who wants Hall Cat?" he asked, leaning down to give Roscoe a pat.

"We're not sure yet," Lolli said. "We need to ask her. But we wanted to get permission from you first."

The man reached out and scratched Hall Cat under the chin. "I suppose that would be all right," he said. "She deserves more attention than we have to give her right now. And I was thinking about what you kids were saying about her being safer living indoors. I'll miss her, though."

"You can still visit her," Janey told him.
"The lady who might want her lives nearby."

"We'll come back and let you know what she says," Lolli promised.

Lolli led the others back to Grandma Madge's house. Brooke answered the door when they knocked. She looked surprised to see them.

"Oh," she said. "It's the whole Pet Rescue Club! Is that an animal you're rescuing?" She reached out to pat Hall Cat.

"Maybe," Lolli said with a smile. "Is Grandma Madge around?"

"I'm here, I'm here." Grandma Madge hurried up behind Brooke. "Oh! What a cute kitty. I've always loved black cats!"

Lolli traded a smile with her friends. "We're glad to hear that," she said. "Because Hall Cat happens to be looking for a new home."

Janey nodded. "She's super friendly."

"And she's not hyper," Zach added. "I doubt she'd ever trip anybody, no matter what her owners say."

Grandma Madge looked a little confused. "Her owners?"

Everyone started talking at once, telling Grandma Madge all about Hall Cat. Meanwhile Hall Cat herself started to wiggle in Zach's arms. He set her down on the stoop. Roscoe leaned forward to sniff at the cat, and she batted him on the nose with her paw. Then she strolled forward between Brooke and Grandma Madge—right into the house!

"Look," Janey said with a laugh. "She's making herself at home already!"

"You little rascal," Grandma Madge exclaimed. She picked up the cat, who immediately started purring. "Oh my, you are a cutie, aren't you?"

"I think she likes you," Lolli said.

Grandma Madge smiled down at the cat.

"Yes. Well, I really wasn't planning on

getting a pet. But…"

Lolli held her breath. Would Grandma Madge agree to take Hall Cat?

"You need company right now, Grandma," Brooke spoke up. "Maybe a cat like this would be perfect."

"Oh, I don't know, Brookie." Grandma Madge was still smiling. "I don't think I could ever live with a pet named Hall Cat."

"You—you couldn't?" Lolli's heart sank.

"Absolutely not." Grandma Madge winked at her. "The first thing I'll have to do is come up with a much nicer name."

It took Lolli a second to realize what she was saying. Then she heard Zach gasp.

"You mean you'll take her?" he exclaimed.

"Why not?" Grandma Madge said. "As Brookie says, I could use the company. Until Roscoe came to visit, I didn't realize how much I'd missed having an animal around the house. And a nice, quiet older cat will be much easier to manage than a dog or a younger animal, especially once Grandpa comes home."

"Hooray!" Lolli cried. "Now the only thing left is to decide what to name her!"

"How about Halloween?" Zach said.

"Veto," Janey declared. "That's a goofy name. Why not just call her Hallie?"

"Hallie," Grandma Madge said thoughtfully. "You know, I think I like that."

"We should go back and tell her old owners the good news," Janey told her friends.

"Don't bother," Grandma Madge said, cuddling Hall Cat. "I know the young couple you mean. I'll walk down there myself and let them know." She smiled. "I've been wanting to see that sweet baby of theirs, anyway."

"Awesome!" Janey said. "I guess it's another happy ending for the Pet Rescue Club."

"This totally rules," Zach exclaimed.

"Yeah," Adam agreed.

Lolli didn't say anything for a second.

She was so happy she thought she might burst. The Pet Rescue Club had helped another animal! Better yet, they'd helped a person at the same time! She was sure Grandma Madge and Hall Cat—no, Hallie— would be much happier now that that the Pet Rescue Club had helped them find each other. She was pretty sure the baby's family would be happier, too.

"This is definitely a happy ending," Lolli said. "For everyone!"

Food for Thought

We share a lot with our pets: our lives, our homes, our love, our deepest secrets. But is it a good idea to share our food?

Not always. Several common foods that are perfectly safe for people can be dangerous or even deadly for our cats, dogs, and other pets. Also, there are some household items and houseplants that pets should never be allowed to chew on or eat. Here are a few examples, but check _aspca.org_ for a more complete list.

- Onions and garlic
- Chocolate
- Coffee
- Avocado (especially dangerous to birds and rodents)
- Grapes and raisins
- Many human medications
- Antifreeze
- Fabric softener sheets
- Amaryllis
- Pothos (a popular houseplant)

Meet the
Real Hallie!

Hall Cat, the kitty in this story, was inspired by a real-life animal rescue story. A black cat named Hallie was left at a shelter in Illinois when she was ten years old. Her previous owners said they didn't have time for her anymore. Luckily, she was adopted by someone who appreciates older cats, and has been a wonderful partner for her new owner ever since!

Look for
the first book in the
**PET RESCUE
CLUB** series!

**Book #1—
A New Home
for Truman**

Animal-crazy Janey can't have any pets of her own because of her father's severe allergies. So Janey creates a blog for kids to post cute photos of their dogs and cats. But when she receives a heartbreaking photo of a skinny, homeless dog, Janey isn't sure what to do. Her friends Lolli, Adam, and Zach get involved to try to help. Can the four of them save the dog— and maybe start a pet rescue club to help other animals in need?